GRANDPA NITWIT

Written and Illustrated by
PAT BRAHS

ISBN 978-1-68526-468-0 (Paperback)
ISBN 978-1-68526-470-3 (Hardcover)
ISBN 978-1-68526-469-7 (Digital)

Covenant Books
11661 Hwy 707
Murrells Inlet, SC 29576
www.covenantbooks.com

mama moose stories

His first attempt at cooking
Sure didn't go all that well.

There's way too much spaghetti.
There's evidence you can tell.

Grandma has a hidden stash
Of candy she's put away.

The visit with the grandkids
Is coming up today.

She checks on her special treats,
but there's none there at all.

"Grandpa, did you eat those treats?"
He says, "I really don't recall."

Grandpa likes to show his skills,
and kite flying would be one.

Too long a tail for his kite.
Kite flying is no longer fun.

FROGGIE FLOAT   MONKEY MANNERS   KLEAN KAT   Tommy   TIDY TURTLE   DIPPER DOGGIE

7

Grandpa truly gets real happy
when offered any ice cream.

Never would he turn it down.
To him it's a perfect dream.

Scoops are big of any flavor
and heaping on a large spoon.

But the clothes that he's wearing,
wash time is coming real soon.

He wants to save some money
when a haircut is overdue.

For sure damage has been done.
A barber he's not, but who knew.

11

He loves the fact when wrestling,
the grandkids are all around.

He feels like an important chief
even though he's underground.

Grandpa NitWit has his fun.
His faces make you merry.

They may look a little strange,
but never are they scary.

*Which Grandpa NitWit's face
looks most like your grandpa?*

Always I have won the game
that's been called tug-of-war.

My wins were always easy,
and my body was never sore.

With all his constant bragging,
something went extremely wrong.

His face molded to the ground,
'cause his strength is no longer strong.

Grandpa has a mighty sneeze
that he wants everyone to hear.

A loud alarming noise is heard
throughout the atmosphere.

Grandpa should be doing his work,
but he likes to read much more.

A hiding place he has found.
Thoughts are erased of any chore.

With his grandson, there's a bet.
"If my team wins, here's the thing."

You must declare, to all the world,
"My grandpa knows everything."

Grandpa has only one pair
of shoes he wears every day.

But at the store, he liked a pair.
Now there's many and that's okay.

Grandma doesn't care to cook.
A can of soup he has to eat.

"Bowl of garbage," Grandpa says.
Garbage ends up under his seat.

He likes to tell his stories
and repeats them many times.

To all who have to listen,
deep sleep wins every time.

The game that Grandpa is watching,
it's his favorite team of all.

The score is six to seven,
And he hates the ref's bad call.

He turns the channel quickly off,
for he can't stand them to lose.

TV gets the entire blame
with Grandpa's loud abuse.

He never finds the right notes
that are in his favorite song.

No one ever guesses his tune,
'cause his notes are always wrong.

Whenever he buys, it's three alike.
The problem is, there's no more room.

He wants really bad, shiny red bikes.
But there's no place for even a broom.

*Great Grandpa NitWit made
an error. He bought four
of a kind instead of three.
Can you find his mistake?*

He dresses up like Santa.
The kids all know he's a fake.

They remember the famous song,
"And be good for goodness sake."

From his clan he wants to know,
"Who stole my favorite hammer?"

"I told you not to touch my things."
And louder became his grammar.

No matter the skills you might have,
Grandpa's proud of your good traits.

"Work really hard," he likes to say.
To him you're always his precious saints.

What trait, or traits, do you have,
that if Grandpa knew, he would
be even more proud of you?

Grandpa plays the game of bingo,
whenever he gets a chance.

His bingo yell is oh so loud,
it's heard from here to France.

He likes to join you in your fun,
and have a special cup of tea.

But best of all, it's in his heart,
with you is where he wants to be.

HELPS

ERASERS   PENCILS

REPAIRS

PROTECTS

COACHES

45

There's times you need Grandpa's help,
whether schoolwork or repairs.

A bit of coaching or some love,
consider it done, 'cause he cares.

He spreads his joy throughout the day.
Wants you happy in every way.

He's silly and funny, gentle and kind.
You're dearest to him, you will find.

ABOUT THE AUTHOR

To all the people around her, it has been extremely important to the author to give them encouragement and kindness and point out their possibilities. Writing and illustrating for children is a way to reach young readers and spread happiness and humor their way.